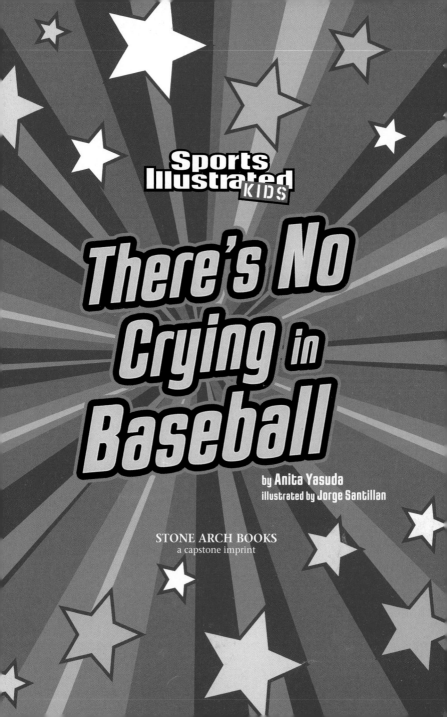

Sports Illustrated KIDS

There's No Crying in Baseball

by Anita Yasuda
illustrated by Jorge Santillan

STONE ARCH BOOKS
a capstone imprint

VICTORY SCHOOL SUPERSTARS

Sports Illustrated KIDS *There's No Crying in Baseball*
is published by Stone Arch Books – A Capstone Imprint
151 Good Counsel Drive, P.O. Box 669
Mankato, Minnesota 56002
www.capstonepub.com

Art Director and Designer: Bob Lentz
Creative Director: Heather Kindseth
Production Specialist: Michelle Biedscheid

Timeline photo credits: Library of Congress (top left & top
right); Damian Strohmeyer (bottom right), David E. Klutho
(middle right), Neil Leifer (bottom left).

Library of Congress Cataloging-in-Publication Data is
available on the Library of Congress website.

ISBN: 978-1-4342-2226-8 (library binding)
ISBN: 978-1-4342-3077-5 (paperback)

Summary: After Tyler sprains his ankle, he does not want to
participate in the spirit activities at school.

Printed in the United States of America in Stevens Point, Wisconsin.
092010   005934WZS11

TABLE of CONTENTS

TYLER TROFEE

Baseball

AGE: 10
GRADE: 4
SUPER SPORTS ABILITY: Super shooter

CARMEN

ALICIA

JOSH

DANNY

KENZIE **TYLER**

VICTORY SCHOOL MAP

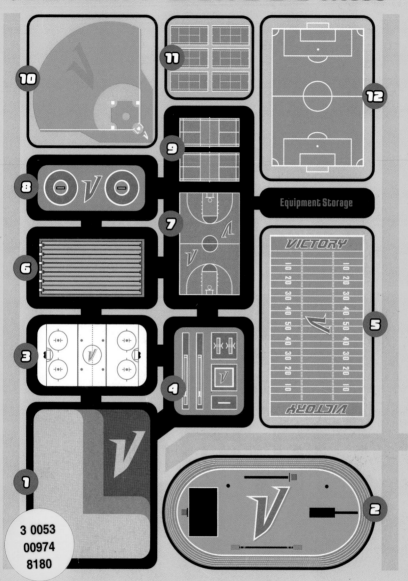

3 0053
00974
8180

1. Main Offices/Classrooms
2. Track and Field
3. Hockey/Figure Skating
4. Gymnastics
5. Football
6. Swimming
7. Basketball
8. Wrestling
9. Volleyball
10. Baseball/Softball
11. Tennis
12. Soccer

A Fierce Pitcher

Whiz! The baseball flies through the hole in the fence. Yes! Next up is the tree across the yard. I deliver the pitch, and the ball rips through the tire swing. In basketball, this would have been a crazy full-court shot.

I have a special skill in basketball. No matter how I shoot, the ball always lands in the hoop. That is why I'm a student at Victory School for Super Athletes. All the students are gifted with a super skill or ability.

After the way I just threw that baseball, I wonder if I could be a fierce pitcher, too.

"Tyler!" Mom shouts. "The World Series will have to wait. You don't want to be late for school . . . again."

"Coming," I yell. I'm on the school's spirit team, and we have a meeting today. I can't be late!

The spirit team helps plan special events at school. We've been really busy the last few weeks because it's Spirit Month. This month, I've spent hours making flags and posters. I even led goofy games at recess. Paper Plate Frisbee was my favorite.

Today the spirit team has to come up with one last event. And I know just what to suggest.

I race down the hall. I can't believe it.
How come I'm always late? I slide into
class just in time to hear the bell sound.
Riiiinnnng!

"Well, that's one way to arrive at a
meeting," says Principal Armstrong,
grinning.

"Sorry, sir," I say. I can feel my face turning red.

"Did you oversleep?" asks my friend Danny. "You need my speed."

Danny is never late for anything in his life. He is super fast. If I had his skill, I could leave home with minutes to spare, toast in one hand, backpack in the other. And I would still be early!

Principal Armstrong hops onto a stool. "Let's get this meeting started," he says.

"Our last spirit event is on ⁻riday," says Kenzie. "But we still don't hav⸍ a plan."

"I have an idea," I say. "W⸍ should challenge the teachers to a game of baseball." Over the past few weeks, I've watched the World Series. My classmates have, too.

Principal Armstrong looks happy.
"Sounds great to me," he says.

"All in favor raise your hand," says
Danny. Everyone raises their hands. "Okay!
It looks like we will be playing against the
teachers!" he says.

"Great! Time to get going, everybody," says Principal Armstrong. "Good meeting."

I head to my locker. Kenzie is waiting for me when I get there. "Did you know that Principal Armstrong played baseball in the big leagues?" she asks.

I shrug, pretending I'm not worried. But she probably can tell that I am.

"I heard that Principal Armstrong is so fast," says Kenzie, "that he can play all of the outfield positions at the same time."

I try not to look surprised, even though I am shocked. "Well, we all have a super skill," I say, hoping that Kenzie doesn't notice the squeak in my voice.

"I guess it's too late now!" she says. She grabs my arm and points at a sign on the wall.

VICTORY SUPERSTARS

STUDENT/TEACHER

BASEBALL GAME!

CHEER FOR YOUR FAVORITE TEAM!

SHOW SCHOOL SPIRIT!
WEAR SCHOOL COLORS!
MAKE A SIGN!
PARENTS WELCOME!

Practice Time

At recess, Kenzie easily carries the equipment, plus the batting cage, onto the field. She has super strength. She could carry almost anything.

"Hey, Kenzie," I shout. "You forgot one."

I pretend Kenzie's pile is a hoop. I toss the ball under my leg. It lands perfectly on top. Maybe I do have a future in baseball!

The spirit team quickly grabs bats, mitts, and balls. No one minds which position they play. I can tell right away it is going to be a good practice.

"How about a low one?" I yell to Danny. He adjusts his cap and tries to look mean.

"Try and catch this one," he shouts.

I dive onto the grass for it. "Yes!" It feels great to be playing ball.

"Another," I shout, moving side to side.

Danny throws again. I see the ball coming. I leap into the air. "Gotcha," I say.

"How about letting me hit a few?" asks a familiar voice. It is Principal Armstrong striding towards us.

"Great," I say.

"Okay, let's do this," Danny yells.

Danny is a blur of movement. Playing next to him is like playing next to a rushing train. My heart is pounding. I don't want to make a mistake in front of Principal Armstrong.

Wham! Smack! Crack! Principal Armstrong is like a machine. He hits balls out left, middle, and right, short and long. Danny and I dive here and leap there. It's crazy fun!

A fly ball soars in my direction. I should run backward, but I make a total newbie mistake. I turn and run for it.

23

Losing sight of the ball, I turn again only to trip over my own two feet.

"Ouch!" I moan as I come down hard. I know something is wrong. My left ankle feels really bad. Everyone rushes over.

"Are you okay?" asks Kenzie, kneeling down on the grass.

"Um, yeah," I lie. "It only hurts a little." Kenzie helps me up. But when I try to walk, the pain shoots up my leg. I'm not fooling anyone.

Principal Armstrong looks concerned. "Let's go see the nurse, Tyler," he says.

I have a feeling that I won't be playing ball tomorrow. I can't believe my bad luck.

Feeling Bad

At dinner, Dad tries to cheer me up. "It's a mild sprain, Tyler," he says. "It'll keep you off the spirit baseball team, but you'll be back at basketball in a week."

"Hmm," I mutter, pushing my potatoes around the plate.

"Hey," Dad teases, "there's no crying in baseball."

"I'm not crying, Dad!" I snap.

"I know, Tyler. I was just joking around. Just take it easy tonight, and you'll feel better in the morning," he says.

Dad doesn't get it. I haven't felt this bad since I got benched for being a ball hog in basketball.

After dinner, I hang out in my room, thinking about how the day was supposed to have turned out.

Pretty soon, Mom knocks on my door and opens it. "Phone call, Tyler," she says. "It's Kenzie."

I don't want to talk to anyone, but I mutter thanks and take the phone anyway. "Hi, Kenzie," I say into the phone.

"Hey, you disappeared after recess," Kenzie says.

"I didn't feel like talking," I snap. The truth is I avoided everyone by hiding out in the nurse's room until Mom picked me up.

"But you are coming tomorrow, right?" Kenzie asks.

"Why bother?" I reply. "What am I going to do?"

"That doesn't sound like the Tyler that I know," Kenzie says, sounding upset.

I don't say anything. I don't want to talk about it. In fact, I don't want to talk about anything at all.

"Who is always planning fun stuff at school like popcorn days?" she asks. "And who came up with the new best day of the week — PJ Day?"

"Me," I admit. Before, I felt disappointed. Now, I feel guilty. I don't want to let down my friends or the school.

"I guess I should go," I say. "Sorry for being a jerk."

"It's okay," Kenzie replies. "So do you have any ideas for tomorrow's pregame show?" she asks.

"You bet," I reply.

We spend the next hour planning. As ideas start to flow, I forget about my ankle. By the time I hang up, I'm really looking forward to tomorrow.

"Mom," I yell, "do we have food coloring?"

A Show of Spirit

"Well," says Ms. Best, my math teacher, "I see that someone is not lacking spirit."

I grin. Mom helped me color my hair red and blue, our school colors. It looks so cool!

It's almost time for the spirit activities to begin. I'm so excited. As I head out to the field, Kenzie gives me a thumbs up.

"See? I knew you would be here," she says.

"Where else would I be?" I reply.

This is my chance to show Victory spirit. I grab the microphone.

"Would the owners of the BMX bike that used to be red, please report to the diamond? You have won the dirtiest bike prize at Victory," I say.

I hold up coupons for a free wash. My class is armed with sponges and buckets of water.

Now it's time for the activities to start. Principal Armstrong, Ms. Best, and some of the students get ready for a tricycle race. "On your marks! Get set! Go!" I yell.

Principal Armstrong's knees are up to his shoulders.

"Come on, Principal Armstrong!" someone shouts.

"Put the pedal to the metal," yells another.

Some of the kids pedal off the track. Coach Field and Coach Pushner crash.

One of the kindergarten kids races by them. I can hardly stand, I am laughing so hard.

The games are working! Everyone is having a great time. I keep the events rolling.

During the egg-and-spoon race, Coach Murphy, my basketball coach, hops on one leg. He even does the chicken dance, and the egg still doesn't fall off.

Aha! Now I know his special skill. His hand acts like a giant magnet. I wish I had that ability.

Coach Murphy raises his arms above his head as he crosses the finish line. You would think he had just won Olympic gold.

"Great job, Coach," I say, giving him a ribbon.

Star Spirit

The kids are really into the big game.
The cheerleaders are leading the crowd
from their seats in the stands.

They yell, "Get up and clap your hands!
Stomp your feet in the stands!"

The student team bats first. Danny steps
up to the plate. Ms. Best pitches a perfect
curve ball.

"Strike one," calls the umpire.

"Come on, Danny!" I shout.

Ms. Best's next pitch is straight out of a textbook, but Danny makes contact. It's a solid hit down the first base line. He's so fast that he actually makes it home!

Our next batter strikes out. Then two doubles, and we have one player home. After two more outs, the teachers are up. Students 2, Teachers 0.

Principal Armstrong is up first for the teachers. He connects on the first pitch and makes it to third.

Next, after two strikes, Coach Field hits a double, bringing Principal Armstrong home. Coach Field leaps from home base to first and on to second. "She has springs in her feet," I say, amazed.

After that, our pitcher manages two more strikeouts. At the end of the game, the students win by one!

"Give yourselves a round of applause," says Principal Armstrong.

"And one for the teachers," I shout. "Hip-hip hooray!"

Principal Armstrong hands out ribbons to each class. Then he holds up a special baton — the Victory Spirit Stick.

"This stick represents the positive spirit of Victory," he says. "The class which displays the most spirit will hang the stick over their classroom door."

The crowd gets super quiet. I cross my fingers. I think our class really deserves it, but everyone showed a lot of spirit today.

Principal Armstrong continues, "All month, our most spirited class wore school colors and participated in the goofy games. Today they worked magic with sponges. Plus, they had a great team leader."

That sounds familiar. Could it be? I wonder, inching forward.

Then I hear him say, "Tyler Trofee and Room 102 win the Spirit Stick for their amazing show of Victory spirit."

My whole class starts cheering.

As I take the stick for our class, I notice what is written on it: Tyler Trofee — Star Spirit. This day could not have gone better. I raise the Spirit Stick above my head and shout, "Go Victory!"

GLOSSARY

ability (uh-BIL-i-tee)—skill or power

challenge (CHAL-uhnj)—to invite or dare to take part in a contest

disappointed (diss-uh-POINT-ed)—let down or without hope

equipment (i-KWIP-muhnt)—the items or tools needed to do a particular thing

fierce (FIHRSS)—extremely active or determined

full-court shot (FUL-kort SHOT)—in basketball, a shot that goes from one end of the court to the other

microphone (MYE-kruh-fone)—an instrument that changes sound into an electric current to make the sound louder

outfield (OUT-feeld)—the area of a baseball field between the foul lines and beyond the infield

participated (par-TISS-uh-pay-ted)—joined with others in an activity or event

BASEBALL IN HISTORY

1839 — Abner Doubleday invents modern baseball in Cooperstown, New York.

1856 — Baseball becomes known as America's national pastime.

1858 — Fans are charged to watch a game for the first time. The fee is fifty cents.

1869 — The first professional team, the **Cincinnati Red Stockings**, is formed.

1927 — **Babe Ruth** becomes the first player to hit sixty home runs in a single season.

1956 — Don Larsen throws the only perfect game in World Series history.

1974 — **Hank Aaron** breaks Babe Ruth's all-time home run record with 715.

1994 — Major league players go on strike. The World Series is canceled.

1998 — **Mark McGwire** and Sammy Sosa race to break the single-season home run record. McGwire does it first and sets a new record of seventy.

2010 — Famed New York Yankee owner George Steinbrenner dies. The **Yankees** won seven World Series under his ownership.

FIRST NINE OF THE
CINCINNATI
(RED STOCKING) BASE BALL CLUB.

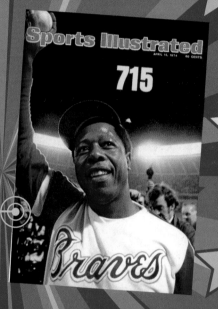

Sports Illustrated

APRIL 15, 1974   60 CENTS

715

VICTORY SCHOOL SUPERSTARS

Five Fouls and You're Out!

It's a Wrestling Mat, Not a Dance Floor

There's a Hurricane in the Pool!

There's No Crying in Baseball

Who Wants to Play Just for Kicks?

You Can't Spike Your Serves

Read them ALL!